How does your garden grow?

Caroline pushed open the door of her room and stood out of the way so Maria could get a good look at her new wallpaper. "This is it!"

Her friend took a step backward. "Wow! Look at all those purple and yellow flowers!"

"Aren't they great?" Caroline carried the popcorn into the room and sat on her bed. "Come on in."

Maria took slow, careful steps as she walked across the room. Caroline realized that her friend had not yet said how much she *liked* the wallpaper. The flowers had probably taken her breath away. Caroline wanted to hear Maria say how beautiful they were, so she said, "What do you really think about my room? Don't you just love the paper?"

"Uh . . ." Maria bit her lower lip. "It's very — interesting."

"Interesting?" That was a word Caroline's mother used when she didn't like something very much but she didn't want to hurt someone's feelings.

"More than interesting," Maria said quickly. "I bet this wallpaper will really grow on me after I've seen it a few more times."

Look for these books in the Caroline Zucker series:

Caroline Zucker
Makes A Big Mistake

by Jan Bradford
Illustrated by Marcy Ramsey

Troll Associates

Library of Congress Cataloging-in-Publication Data

Bradford, Jan.
  Caroline Zucker makes a big mistake / by Jan Bradford;
illustrated by Marcy Ramsey.
    p.   cm.
  Summary: After insisting that the redecoration of her bedroom
include wallpaper with lavender daisies and yellow roses, nine-year-
old Caroline changes her mind but cannot figure out what to do
about her colorful mistake.
  ISBN 0-8167-2023-1 (lib. bdg.)   ISBN 0-8167-2024-X (pbk.)
  [1. Bedrooms—Fiction. 2. Interior decoration—Fiction.]
I. Ramsey, Marcy Dunn, ill. II. Title.
PZ7.B7228Catf 1991
[Fic]—dc20   90-11160

A TROLL BOOK, published by Troll Associates,
Mahwah, NJ 07430

Copyright © 1991 by Troll Associates, Mahwah, New Jersey

All rights reserved. No part of this book may be used or
reproduced in any manner whatsoever without written
permission from the publisher.

Printed in the United States of America.

10 9 8 7 6 5 4 3 2 1

WHO WANTS RABBITS ON THEIR WALLS?

"A family meeting?" Patricia Zucker looked up at her older sister. "Caroline, are we in trouble?"

Now that Caroline was nine years old, her sisters seemed to expect her to know everything. But she had no idea why their parents had called a surprise family council meeting Saturday morning right after breakfast. "I don't know. Did you forget to hang up your towel after your bath last night?"

"Not me." Patricia turned to their six-year-old sister Vicki. "Did you leave the cap off the toothpaste again?"

Vicki's brown curls bounced as she shook her head. "No, I didn't," she insisted.

"Then why do we need a meeting?" Patricia was still worried.

"Maybe Mom and Dad have *good* news," Caroline said, trying to look on the bright side.

"Maybe we're going to have a new baby!" Vicki smiled. Her kindergarten teacher was going to have a baby and now Vicki thought everyone should have one.

"Do you think that's it?" Patricia asked.

Caroline just crossed her fingers behind her back and hoped Vicki was wrong. Having two pesky little sisters who liked to play dress-up with her clothes was quite enough, in her opinion. She didn't need another sister—or a brother.

Their mother came into the kitchen with a pad of paper and a pen in her hand. That meant they were going to vote on something, so Caroline knew the meeting had nothing to do with a baby. You didn't vote on things like that. She sighed with relief.

"What are we going to talk about?" she asked her mother.

Mrs. Zucker smiled as if she were happy about something, but she kept it a secret.

"Let's wait for your father," she said.

"*Dad!*" Patricia shouted. She wasn't very patient about waiting for people.

A second later, Mr. Zucker was standing in the kitchen doorway. "Did someone call me?"

"Sit down, Daddy," Vicki told him, pointing to a chair. He hurried to his side of the table, pretending that Vicki had scolded him. After he sat down, he folded his hands on the table and looked at Vicki. "Why have you called this meeting, little one?"

Vicki giggled, showing off the space where her two front baby teeth used to be. "It's not *my* meeting, Daddy. It's yours."

He glanced across the table at Mrs. Zucker. "You know, I believe she's right. Shall we get started?"

Their mother took the cap off her pen so she'd be ready to write. "You tell them," she said to Mr. Zucker.

"We got a check in the mail yesterday—" he began.

"Did we win a contest?" Caroline asked eagerly. She remembered seeing a television show about somebody who had won ten million dollars. She started to get out of her chair. Maybe the TV people were waiting outside with their cameras and microphones!

"Nothing like that," Mr. Zucker said before anyone could get too excited. Caroline sat back down while her father explained, "Your mother and I bought stock in a company last year. Now the company has been sold, and the new owners sent us a check to buy the stock back from us."

Vicki squinted at him. "What's stock?"

"It's a piece of paper that says you own part

3

of a company. But that's not important right now. What matters is the check and what we're going to do with it."

"Wonder World!" Caroline cried, naming a famous theme park in Texas.

"No!" Patricia sat up tall. "I want to see the ocean."

"Which one?" their mother teased.

Patricia shrugged her shoulders. "I don't care. Any ocean."

"Could I get that big stuffed Snuggle Kitten in the We-Love-Toys store window?" Vicki opened her brown eyes wide and looked from her mother to her father. She loved the Snuggle Kittens almost as much as she loved her family, Caroline thought.

"Wait!" Mrs. Zucker held up her hands like a policeman stopping traffic.

Mr. Zucker explained, "Your mother and I discussed this last night and we decided to use the money for something the whole family can enjoy. We came up with two ideas. We could buy a new tent and camping gear. . . ."

"Or we could redecorate all the bedrooms in our house," Mrs. Zucker finished.

"Bedrooms!" all three girls yelled at once.

Mrs. Zucker smiled and put the cap back on her pen. She said to Mr. Zucker, "I told you we wouldn't need to vote."

Their father sighed. "Why do you *women* al-

4

ways stick together? Don't any of you want to go camping with me?"

"And sleep on the ground?" Caroline wrinkled her nose. "I'd rather have a new bed for my room. A *canopy* bed!"

"Me, too," Patricia cried.

"I want bunk beds in our room," Vicki said to her sister. "And I get to sleep on top!"

"There isn't enough money to buy furniture," Mrs. Zucker told them. "But we could buy new wallpaper for each room."

"Oh," Patricia said. She looked disappointed. So did Vicki.

But Caroline was already making plans. New wallpaper! All right! Her room needed a change. The candy-cane-and-peppermint-ball wallpaper had been fine when she was a little kid. She had picked it because it made her think of her Grandpa Nevelson's candy store. But a nine-year-old girl needed something more grown-up.

"Can I go to Maria's house this morning?" she asked her mother. Her best friend's mother, Mrs. Santiago, had magazines full of pictures of beautiful rooms. Besides looking at the magazines, Caroline wanted to share her exciting news with Maria.

"Now?" Mrs. Zucker asked in surprise. "I thought we'd go to Fred's Home Store right away to choose our wallpaper."

Vicki clapped her hands. She wasn't disappointed anymore. "Let's go!"

"What's the hurry?" Caroline asked. Maria's mother knew almost as much about decorating as she did about making clothes. She designed the costumes for the Stratford Theater in their town—Homestead, Colorado. Caroline really wanted to get Mrs. Santiago's advice before she went wallpaper shopping.

Mrs. Zucker pointed to the morning paper that was still lying on the table. "Fred's Home Store has a big sale. I want to get there before the place gets too crowded."

Mr. Zucker clapped his hands together. "Let's hit the road, ladies."

Half an hour later, Vicki squealed, "Caroline, *look!*" from the far end of the wallpaper counter at Fred's Home Store.

Caroline sighed and closed the sample book she'd been checking. This was the fourth time Vicki had called her. Finally, Mrs. Zucker told Caroline to *please* look at whatever Vicki wanted to show her.

Caroline didn't really mind joining her sister. She had looked through five books and she hadn't found the *right* wallpaper yet. The books were big, heavy things filled with samples of real wallpaper. There were hundreds of patterns. Choosing one of them was a much harder job than she had expected.

"What do you want to show me?" she asked Vicki.

Vicki's chubby finger pointed to a pale pink paper covered with cute little white-and-blue cartoon bunnies.

"It's so . . . babyish," Caroline said.

Patricia peered over Vicki's shoulder. "Well, I like it."

Caroline wrinkled her nose. She was surprised that Patricia, who was almost seven years old, agreed with little Vicki. That paper was about as silly as the candy-cane wallpaper in her own room back home.

"It's better than the A-B-C, one-two-three paper we have now," Patricia pointed out.

Caroline admitted that Patricia was right. The bunnies were a *tiny* bit better.

"What have you picked?" Patricia asked her.

"Nothing yet."

The girls looked over at the table where their parents were discussing which wallpaper to buy for their own room. It looked as if they were ready to make a decision.

"You'd better hurry," Patricia warned. "When Mom and Dad make up their minds, they'll want to buy everything and go home."

Caroline raced back to her seat. If she looked very carefully this time, she knew she could

7

find a paper she liked before her parents were ready to leave.

She opened one more of the huge sample books. The first six pages showed stripes in different colors. Boring, she decided. The next group of pages showed a pattern full of diamonds and X's. When Caroline stared at it too long, it made her dizzy.

Quickly, she flipped the pages until she reached the center of the book. Caroline suddenly sucked in her breath. There it was—the perfect wallpaper for her attic bedroom!

"I've found it!" she called.

She spun around in her seat and smiled at her mother. With so many sample books to choose from, it hadn't been easy finding the right paper, but she'd done it without any help. Caroline felt very proud.

Vicki hopped off her chair and raced to Caroline's side. She stood on tiptoe to get a clear view of the wallpaper sample. She blinked twice and then said, "Yuck!"

"Yuck?" Patricia asked as she came up behind Vicki. "It can't be *that* bad."

Caroline happily showed her the pattern she had selected. It was a design of huge lavender daisies and yellow roses.

Patricia didn't say anything at first. Then she made a gagging sound in her throat.

Caroline punched her in the arm. "Grow up!

This isn't little kid stuff like your bunny rabbits."

The comments made their parents curious. They left their table to see Caroline's choice for themselves. They looked at it for a long time. Then Mrs. Zucker rested a hand on Caroline's shoulder. She sounded very serious as she said, "If you choose this wallpaper, Caroline, remember that you're going to have to live with it for a long time."

Her father made a noise that sounded as if he was trying to swallow a laugh. When he could finally talk, he said, "I hate to say this, but honey, that's really *ugly.*"

Vicki and Patricia giggled, but Caroline ignored them all. What did any of them know? The lavender-and-yellow flowered wallpaper was exactly what she needed. If both her little sisters and her parents hated it, then it had to be perfect for a nine-year-old girl.

2

LAVENDER DAISIES AND YELLOW ROSES

"What's wrong with you?" Maria asked Caroline during recess the following Friday afternoon. "You haven't beeen able to stand still all day."

"The men are putting up my new wallpaper today—maybe right now! I wish I could go home and watch them." Caroline bounced up and down while they waited for their turn at kickball.

Maria sighed. "You're so lucky. I'd like to redecorate my room."

Caroline couldn't understand why Maria would want to change anything about her super bedroom. She even had a skylight in her ceiling so she could watch the moon and the stars at night! But she just said, "I guess I'm pretty lucky."

Next to them, Duncan Fairbush was showing

off a big scab on his elbow. "I must have been going a hundred miles an hour when my bike tire exploded," he bragged to anyone who would listen.

"A hundred miles an hour?" Caroline repeated scornfully. "Get real, Duncan!"

He turned and glared at her. She glared right back into his blue eyes, refusing to be the first one to blink. Duncan Fairbush was the biggest pain in the third grade. In fact, he was probably the biggest pain in all of Hart Elementary.

Duncan folded his arms across his skinny chest. "What do you know about fast bikes, Zucker? I bet you still use training wheels! I bet you never even take your bike out of your driveway! Remember the time you flew over the handlebars and hit your face on the road?"

"That happened in *first grade*," Caroline reminded him angrily. "Besides, it was a new bike. I wasn't used to it."

"You sure looked awful," Samantha Collins said, smoothing her long, blond hair. "You had a black eye and a big, ugly scrape across your nose."

Caroline remembered, all right. How could she forget? Her father had even taken a picture of her with her scraped nose and purple eye. He'd taped it to the wall over his workbench in the basement. For some reason he seemed to like it better than any of her school pictures,

11

where her hair was combed perfectly and her face was squeaky clean.

"I guess I know how fast my bike can go," Duncan said, turning everybody's attention back to himself. He shoved his elbow at Caroline. "You can't get a cut like *this* one biking with a bunch of sissy girls."

Caroline backed away. "I don't ride with *sissies*. I could race you any day and I bet I'd win."

He leaned closer to her and scowled. "Oh yeah?"

Caroline scowled back. "Yeah!"

"Class!" Mrs. Nicks, their teacher, called from the door. "Time to come inside."

Caroline started toward the school and bumped into Kevin Sutton. She and Duncan were surrounded by the kids in their class, and that meant everyone had heard Duncan hint that she was a wimp. How did Duncan always make her look like a dope? Grabbing Maria's hand, Caroline began to push her way through the crowd.

But Duncan wouldn't let her leave without having the last word. "We'll finish this Monday," he yelled as the whole group started going into the school.

Caroline sighed and turned to Maria. "What's he going to do? Bring his bike to school and ride around the playground, trying to impress everybody with how fast he can go?"

"Maybe." Then Maria grinned. "Does your dad have one of those things that tells how fast he's running?"

"Yeah . . . he clips it on his belt when he goes jogging." Caroline smiled as she figured out Maria's idea. "I bet I could borrow it. Then we could sneak it onto Duncan's bike somehow and *prove* he can't ride a hundred miles an hour!"

Maria and Caroline raised their right hands high over their heads and slapped their palms together.

"Watch out, Duncan Fairbush," Maria whispered.

Caroline grinned. "Boy, is he going to be embarrassed on Monday!"

But Duncan was the farthest thing from Caroline's mind when she rushed into the house after school that day. She had run all the way from the bus stop, and she didn't stop running until she hurried up the stairs. Then she stopped at the top of the steps and closed her eyes.

She couldn't wait to see how the new wallpaper looked in her room. At the same time, she was nervous. What if it didn't look as wonderful as she'd imagined? Slowly, she took the last

14

few steps to the open door of her bedroom. Then she sucked in a deep breath and opened her eyes.

There were lavender and yellow flowers everywhere; even on the slanted ceiling that started low by the window and got higher and higher until it met the wall on the other side of her room. When she went inside, Caroline felt as if she'd walked into a garden in the middle of summer. All that was missing was a fat bumblebee. She half expected her room to smell like roses, but instead, it smelled like wallpaper paste.

A door slammed downstairs and Caroline heard her sisters' voices. Patricia was probably complaining because she hadn't waited for her at the bus stop. But Patricia and Vicki weren't nearly as excited as Caroline was about the redecorating. She would apologize to them later . . . much later, after she'd had time to enjoy her beautiful new room all by herself.

She wanted to toss her backpack onto her bed, but it was in the middle of her room along with her dresser and desk. They were all covered with a big white cloth. That morning, her father had moved the furniture in each bedroom so the men could work on the walls, and then he had covered everything so nothing would get dirty. Caroline had carefully carried her goldfish down to the kitchen so Justin and

Esmerelda wouldn't be frightened by the workmen.

Caroline threw her backpack into the hall to get it out of her way. Rubbing her chin, she imagined her furniture back in place. Her bed had been in the center of one wall. Her mirror and dresser belonged near her closet. The table that Grandpa Nevelson had made went in the corner. And the desk had been next to the window.

"Wait a minute!" she said out loud. "They don't have to go back into their boring old places. I want everything *different* in my new room!"

She went to the top of the stairs and yelled, "LAURIE!"

When she heard footsteps pounding up the stairs, she knew Laurie Morrell was on her way. Laurie was in Mr. Zucker's history class at Homestead High School. She came to the Zuckers' house nearly every afternoon to stay with the girls until their parents got home from work.

Laurie was out of breath when she dashed into the room and asked, "What is it, Caroline? Are you hurt?"

Caroline smiled. "I'm fine."

"You screamed like it was an emergency," Laurie said. She sounded annoyed.

"It's not an emergency, but it *is* important,"

Caroline told her. "Can you help me move my bed and stuff? I want to rearrange my furniture."

Laurie smiled and pushed up the sleeves of her red sweater. "I *love* rearranging furniture! Let's go."

Together, they pushed the bed against the far wall, where the ceiling was very low. Caroline lay down on the bed to see how it felt to be looking up at the flowered wallpaper. It was almost like having a canopy!

"You'll have to be careful not to bump your head," Laurie warned her.

Caroline sat up and raised her arms over her head. Her fingertips touched the ceiling. "It'll be okay."

"Where do you want the dresser?" Laurie asked.

"Next to my bed," Caroline decided.

They slid the dresser into place and then moved the desk to the opposite wall. The only piece of furniture they didn't move was the table that Grandpa Nevelson had made for Caroline. That was where she kept Justin and Esmerelda's bowl. It stayed in the corner under the eaves.

Laurie brushed her hands against her jeans. "I guess that's it. Do you think you can handle the rest by yourself?"

Caroline still needed to put her belongings

back on her dresser and desk. And the stuffed animals on her bed were all in a heap—they had to be set up in a neat row. "Sure," she said. "Thanks for helping me, Laurie."

"It was fun." Laurie glanced around the room. "I hope you're going to like your new wallpaper." She sounded doubtful.

But Caroline felt all warm and bubbly inside as she said, "I already *love* it!"

As soon as Laurie left, Caroline plugged the tape player into the wall and popped her new Lucy Hanson tape into it. She sang along with Lucy as she set her jewelry box on top of her dresser. Then she arranged her pencils, markers, notebooks and sketch pad on the desk top. She rested her bulletin board against the wall so her father could hang it later.

Caroline finished her work before the tape was over. She sat on the edge of her bed and wished someone would come upstairs to admire her room. She could hardly wait for her parents to get home so she could show it to them. She wished she could call Maria and invite her over, but Maria was visiting her grandmother and she wouldn't be home until Sunday afternoon. That left Patricia and Vicki.

Caroline trotted down the stairs to the bedroom her sisters shared. Their door was closed. She knocked and called, "Hey, Patricia and Vicki. Want to see my room?"

18

Patricia opened the door a crack and stuck her head out, frowning. "You didn't wait for me at the bus stop," she said.

Caroline sighed. "I'm sorry. But I couldn't wait to get home to see my room. It's all fixed up now. Come and see it!"

From inside, Vicki said, "You have to see *our* room first."

Patricia opened the door and Caroline went in. She had to step over the coloring books and toys that were scattered on the floor.

"We're cleaning up," Patricia explained.

Vicki ignored the mess on the floor and pointed to their bright new walls. "Isn't it neat?"

The blue-and-white bunnies hopping across the pale pink wallpaper were pretty cute, Caroline had to admit. She was amazed to see how nice her sisters' room looked without hand prints and crayon scribbles on the wall. "I like it," she said. But she didn't want them to think she liked their room better than her own, so she added, "It's not what I would want, but it looks great in here. Anybody want to see *my* room now?"

Vicki waved her hand in the air. "I do!"

Patricia sighed. "This isn't school, Vicki. You don't have to raise your hand."

"Don't fight, guys. Just come upstairs." Caro-

19

line started back to her room, and both her sisters followed.

Before Vicki and Patricia reached the open door, she told them, "Close your eyes!"

When both girls had done as she asked, Caroline led them inside. She stopped in the very center of her bedroom. "Now you can look!"

Neither Patricia nor Vicki said a thing when they opened their eyes. They stared at the walls in total silence.

Caroline couldn't stand to wait another second. "What do you think?"

"I've never seen so many flowers," Patricia said. "There are too many to count!"

"Aren't they great?" Caroline asked.

Vicki crossed her eyes. "They make me dizzy!"

"Then we better go back downstairs," Patricia said quickly. She grabbed Vicki's hand and they rushed out of Caroline's room.

When they were halfway down the stairs, Caroline heard Vicki say, "I like our bunnies *a lot* better."

"Me, too," Patricia admitted. "But don't tell Caroline."

Caroline smiled. When her sisters were nine, they would understand.

That night the whole family went out for pizza.

"I'm stuffed," Mr. Zucker said after his fifth slice. He sat back in his chair.

"Thanks for bringing us to Tony's Pizza Pie, Dad," Caroline said. She loved the way Tony arranged the sausage pieces into a happy face on the pizza. But he only did it for people he knew and liked. It made Caroline feel that her family was special.

"We were all tired after putting our rooms back into shape," her father said. "I didn't want your mother to cook dinner tonight."

"We love our room," Vicki told him.

"I'm happy with ours, too," Mrs. Zucker said. "It almost seems like a brand-new room . . . all warm and cozy."

"Warm and cozy?" Mr. Zucker shook his head, pretending to be sad. "We could have bought a tent and gone camping. But now all we have is a cozy bedroom."

"I thought you liked it." Mrs. Zucker sounded disappointed.

He slid his arm around her shoulders and gave her a hug, right there in Tony's Pizza Pie. "I like it. But it's fun to tease you."

"What about *my* room?" Caroline asked before her parents could get mushy.

"Your room . . ." Her father seemed to be searching for just the right thing to say. At last he said, "Your new wallpaper reminds me of one time when I stayed overnight with my

21

grandmother. She had wallpaper a lot like yours in her guest room."

He didn't say whether or not it was good that her wallpaper made him think of visiting Great-grandmother Zucker, but Caroline decided that that was what he meant. She smiled and said, "Thanks, Dad."

It must have been a compliment. How could anyone *not* like her room? It was the most colorful one in the whole house!

3

THE AMAZING FLYING BIKE

"I can't wait to see how your room looks," Maria said on Sunday afternoon as she and Caroline headed upstairs.

"Don't spill your soda," Caroline warned. "If we make a mess, my mom won't let me have popcorn and drinks in my room ever again until I'm at least fifteen."

Maria giggled. "Your mom's not that strict."

"She gets pretty upset when anyone spills something," Caroline told her.

"So does my mom. Especially if they spill it on the white carpet in our living room."

At the top of the stairs, Caroline declared, "When I have kids, I'm going to let them eat anyplace they want to."

"Me, too." Maria nodded and her long, dark hair almost dipped into the two glasses of soda she was carrying.

Caroline balanced the popcorn bowl on her hip and reached for her doorknob. "Are you ready?"

Maria nodded eagerly. "I'm ready."

Caroline pushed the door open and stood out of the way so Maria could get a good look. "This is it!"

Her friend took a step backward. "Wow! Look at all those flowers!"

"I know. Aren't they great?" Caroline carried the popcorn into the room and sat on her bed. But Maria was still standing in the doorway with their drinks. Caroline called, "Come on in."

Maria took slow, careful steps as she walked across the room. It reminded Caroline of the time they had tried not to step on any cracks in the sidewalk for a whole day.

"Why are you walking like that?" she asked. "Are you worried about spilling the soda?"

"I feel like I'm walking through a garden. I don't want to step on any flowers—or snakes, or worms," Maria explained.

Caroline giggled. "I don't have snakes or worms in my room—just my goldfish. Besides, the flowers are only on the walls."

Maria set the drinks on the dresser and sat cross-legged on the bed. She couldn't seem to stop looking around the room, from one wall to another and then up at the sloping ceiling.

Finally, she said, "You sure must like purple-and-yellow flowers."

"I didn't know how much I liked them until I saw this wallpaper in the sample book." Caroline felt very grown-up, talking about how she had chosen the paper all by herself.

Maria kept looking around. "I can't imagine sleeping in a room like . . ." Instead of finishing her sentence, she stuffed a handful of popcorn into her mouth.

Caroline realized that her friend had not yet said how much she *liked* the wallpaper. The flowers had probably taken her breath away. Caroline wanted to hear Maria say how beautiful they were, so she said, "What do you really think about my room?"

Maria swallowed hard. "I like the way you rearranged your furniture. Putting your bed in this corner was a great idea. It's almost like having a canopy."

"That's what I thought." Caroline waited for Maria to talk about the wallpaper. When she didn't, Caroline said, "What about the walls? Don't you just love the paper?"

"Uh . . ." Maria bit her lower lip. "It's very— interesting."

"*Interesting?*" That was a word Caroline's mother used when she didn't like something very much but she didn't want to hurt someone's feelings.

25

"*More* than interesting," Maria said quickly. "I bet this wallpaper will really grow on me after I've seen it a few more times."

Caroline hopped off the bed and turned on the radio. She didn't want to talk about her room anymore. It was obvious that Maria didn't like her beautiful wallpaper, but she was too nice to say so.

Maria looked uncomfortable. She was chewing her fingernails, and she hadn't done that since second grade.

Then Caroline heard the first few bars of the next song on the radio, and turned up the volume. "Listen, Maria!" she cried. "It's Roddy Hastings!"

Maria glanced at Caroline through her long, dark eyelashes. When she saw her friend smiling, she smiled, too. "Isn't Roddy adorable?"

"Have you seen the pictures of him in *Rock Times*?" Caroline asked, naming a magazine devoted to rock stars.

"Sure. But if you still have your copy, I'd love to see them again." Maria's cheeks got pink, and Caroline knew she was thinking about Roddy's cute smile and his dimples.

"Still have it? I'll keep it forever!"

Caroline opened her top desk drawer and took out the magazine. She sat close to Maria on the bed, so they could look at the pictures together. Both girls wiped their hands on their jeans before they opened it. It would be *terrible* if they smeared popcorn butter on Roddy Hastings's face.

"He's *so* cute!" Maria sighed when they turned to the photograph of Roddy winking over his shoulder.

"I bet everyone who looks at that picture thinks he's winking at them," Caroline said. That was how *she* felt when she looked at it.

"Watch this," Maria told her. She lifted the picture high enough so she and the picture of Roddy were looking into each other's eyes. Then she winked back at him.

"And he's not just cute," said Caroline, the Roddy Hastings expert. "His songs are good, too."

Maria whispered, "Do you like him better than Lucy Hanson?"

Caroline had asked herself the same question. It seemed that she and Maria had been Lucy Hanson fans forever. She knew she'd never forget Lucy, but . . .

"I like them differently," Caroline explained. "We know all the words to Lucy's songs. We know all her dances from the videos. And when I'm old enough to wear make-up, I plan to look exactly like her."

"I know what you mean," Maria said. "Lucy's my favorite *girl* singer in the world, but

Roddy's my favorite guy. Sometimes I dream about meeting him."

"You do?" Maria had never told her that before. "What happens when you meet him in your dreams?"

Maria's cheeks turned even pinker. "He smiles at me. Then he asks me to dance with him. And he looks even cuter than he does in these pictures!"

"Let's race from the top of Mountain Road down to the park," Caroline said a half-hour later. She had suggested going for a bike ride because the daisies and roses on her walls seemed to be making Maria nervous. And Mountain Road was one of the biggest hills around—which made it lots of fun to ride on.

"Think your bike can go a hundred miles an hour?" Maria teased, reminding Caroline of Duncan's claim.

"A hundred?" Caroline scoffed. "On this hill, I can probably go *two hundred and fifty* miles an hour!"

"Is that all?" Maria laughed. "Then I'll beat you, because *my* bike can race up to *three hundred* miles an hour!"

Caroline squirmed on the seat of her old, red bike until she was comfortable. "No way, Maria Santiago! I'll be at the park before you even get started."

"No way, Caroline Zucker!" Maria hunched over her handlebars. Then she shouted, "Ready . . . set . . . *go!*"

Caroline pedaled hard to build up speed. She loved going faster and faster. The afternoon breeze felt cool on her face, and her hair flew out behind her. Wouldn't Duncan have a fit if he could see them racing down the hill? Caroline wished he was watching. Then he wouldn't make any more jokes about her using training wheels on her bike, or being afraid to ride any farther than her own driveway.

All of a sudden Caroline realized that Maria wasn't next to her anymore. Caroline peered over her shoulder and discovered that she had raced far ahead of her friend, even though Maria was riding the new green bike her parents had given her for her birthday.

Caroline called out, "Hey, Maria! Is that the fastest you can—"

Suddenly her bike hit something and shot up into the air. As Caroline fell, she remembered how much it had hurt when she scraped her face in the first-grade accident. She didn't want to do *that* again, so she kept her head high.

"Ooh!" The sound was forced out of her as she hit the ground. A second later, Maria was leaning over her.

"Are you all right?" Maria's dark eyes were filled with concern.

29

Caroline took a minute to think about it. Her head hadn't hit the sidewalk, but her right arm hurt. And her right leg was starting to throb. Caroline looked over at her bike lying by the curb. It was all bent and twisted.

"Are you hurt?" Maria asked anxiously.

Caroline slowly raised her arm so they could both inspect the damage. "I think this is just a scratch," she said in a wobbly voice.

But Maria looked as if the cut was the grossest thing she'd ever seen.

Caroline tried to ignore her friend's expression. She knew if she started feeling sorry for herself, she might do something dumb—like cry. Instead, she pointed to her right leg. "My leg hurts more than my arm."

"Can you walk?"

"Of course." Caroline wasn't going to let a few cuts and bruises keep her from walking home. But she dreaded telling her parents she had wrecked her bike.

Maria sighed with relief. "Let's go, then."

Telling herself to be brave, Caroline tried to stand up. A horrible pain shot from her ankle up to her knee.

"OW!" she cried, falling back to the sidewalk. "I can't get up. I guess I'm hurt worse than I thought." She wished she were home already. Her mother was a nurse—she always knew what to do to make things better.

31

Maria's face went pale. "Is your leg broken?"

Images of crutches and plaster casts flashed through Caroline's head. Vicki's little friend Mandy had broken her arm last summer and she'd had a pale pink cast. Maybe Caroline could get a purple one.

A woman came out of the nearest house. She hurried over to the girls and asked, "What's the problem?"

Caroline hoped the woman wasn't angry because they were cluttering up the sidewalk. "I fell off my bike," she said. "And now I can't walk."

The woman bent down and took Caroline's hand. Her face was kind.

"It's going to be all right," she told her in a soothing voice. She pointed to her house. "I live right over there. If you'll tell me your phone number, I'll call your mom or dad to come and get you."

"Thank you." Caroline's voice was shaky as she recited the numbers. When the woman had gone, she told Maria, "I sure hope my parents get here soon."

"Me, too." Maria shifted from one foot to the other. "I feel like I should be doing something to help you, but I don't know what."

"Just talk to me." Caroline winced as another pain shot up her leg. Softly, she said, "Maria? You know what? I'm scared."

*　　*　　*

Two hours later, Maria had gone home and Caroline was sitting on a bed behind a white curtain in the hospital emergency room. Her mother was with her, and her father was in the waiting room trying to calm down Patricia and Vicki.

"How much longer?" Caroline asked her mother. It seemed as if the accident had happened last week and she'd been waiting in the emergency room ever since. "What if I was *bleeding?* I could have bled to death by now," she complained.

"If you were bleeding to death, you would have been a *real* emergency and someone would have taken care of you quickly," Mrs. Zucker said to her. "Right now, we're waiting for the X-rays."

As if she had said the magic word, the curtain opened and there was Dr. Reynolds. He smiled at Caroline and said, "You're a very lucky girl."

Lucky? In Caroline's opinion, a lucky girl wouldn't have hit a bump in the sidewalk and flown off her bike.

"When you fell, you could easily have broken your ankle," the doctor said. "But all you have is a mild sprain."

"Are you sure it's just a sprain?" Mrs. Zucker asked. The doctor looked at her in surprise, and she blushed. "I know you're the doctor, but I am a nurse, and—well, my daughter doesn't complain unless something really hurts."

Caroline felt pride swelling inside her chest. Her mother thought she was brave!

"I'm not saying she's not hurt," Dr. Reynolds explained. "It's not a bad sprain, but it must be quite painful. I'm going to wrap it before you leave, and . . ."

"When we get home, keep the leg elevated and put ice on it," Mrs. Zucker finished for him. "For how long?"

"The sprain needs time to heal." The doctor rubbed his chin. "I'd recommend you keep her off her feet for a few days . . . at least until Wednesday."

Caroline groaned. She couldn't walk until *Wednesday*? What about Monday and Tuesday when she was supposed to be at school? She'd been looking forward to getting crutches so she could hobble into class the next morning. But now she wouldn't be able to do anything at all for two whole days! What could be more boring than that?

4

A PICNIC AND A FROG

But on Monday morning, Caroline decided that staying home wasn't going to be so bad after all. Her father had gone to work. Patricia and Vicki had left for school. And her mother had taken the morning off so she could take care of Caroline.

Because she had to stay off her feet, Caroline wasn't even allowed to come downstairs. But that was all right. She would be spending the next two days in her beautiful new room. A big sofa pillow was resting under Caroline's right foot so the ankle was higher than the rest of her leg. Her mother had tucked two more sofa pillows behind Caroline's back so she could sit up comfortably.

And best of all, before he left that morning her father had brought her the television set from her parents' bedroom. It was color and it had a remote control. While Maria and Samantha and all the rest of the kids in Mrs. Nicks' third-grade class were doing math problems at ten o'clock, Caroline would be watching Lucy Hanson. She was going to be a guest on Tom Sullivan's talk show. What a great day to be stuck at home!

Her mother poked her head into Caroline's room. "How are you doing, honey?"

With her ankle wrapped in a bandage and her foot on the sofa pillow, Caroline didn't hurt at all. "I'm fine," she said.

"Can I get you anything?"

"Could you give me my schoolbag, please?" Caroline asked.

"Are you going to do homework? What a good idea!"

"I might try to catch up on my reading assignment." Caroline had planned to read the two chapters last night, but she hadn't felt up to it. She figured she might do some reading after the cartoons and Lucy Hanson.

"I'm impressed," Mrs. Zucker told her. "I thought you'd be fooling around all day."

Caroline pointed at her foot. "There's not much I can do."

Her mother sat on the edge of the bed. "Honey, would you mind if I went out for a while?"

Caroline pouted. "I thought you could stay

home this morning." She didn't expect her mother to spend every minute with her, but she hadn't expected her to go out right away, either.

"I'll be back soon," Mrs. Zucker promised. "There are just a few quick errands I need to run. Can I get you anything while I'm out?"

"How about some soda and candy from Grandpa Nevelson's store?" Caroline asked.

Mrs. Zucker leaned over and kissed her forehead. "Since you're being such a good sport about all this, I think you deserve some treats."

"Thanks, Mom." Caroline wondered why she hadn't thought of spraining her ankle before. It was great! Her parents were giving her anything she wanted. They weren't mad about her wrecking her bike. And as long as she kept her foot up on the pillow, her ankle didn't even hurt.

It was almost noon when Caroline looked up from her reading book to see her grandfather standing at her bedroom door. He was holding a stack of trays. On the top tray were three soup bowls and a plate full of grilled cheese sandwiches.

"I thought you might like to have lunch with an old friend," he said, smiling.

"I'd love it! But who's minding the store?"

"Mrs. White is taking care of things for a little while," Grandpa Nevelson told her.

"Mrs. White?" Caroline knew the lady who helped her grandfather on weekends and busy holidays. But today was just a regular old Monday. "Why is she there now?"

"I told her my granddaughter needed me," Grandpa Nevelson said with a wink.

Caroline grinned at him. "Where's my mom? Or are we going to eat alone?"

"She'll be up in a minute." He put the tray down on the dresser next to Caroline's bed. Grandpa Nevelson pulled her desk chair close to the bed and sat down. Then he looked around the room for the first time. "You've made some changes, I see," he said.

"I've got new wallpaper," Caroline said proudly. "Do you like it?"

Her grandfather took a long time before he answered her question. "It certainly is . . . colorful."

Was that better or worse than Maria saying it was *interesting?* Caroline wondered. "I like it a lot," she said. "I can pretend I'm sleeping in a garden."

"With the spiders and gnats?" he teased, just the way Maria had.

She shook her head. "There aren't any spiders or gnats in my special garden."

"Then what do the birds eat?"

"Grandpa!" Caroline tried to give him a stern

look, but she couldn't help giggling. "Are you picking on me?"

Just then her mother came into the room. "Dad, are you teasing Caroline?"

Grandpa Nevelson looked very innocent. "Me? I wouldn't tease a poor, injured child. We were just discussing Caroline's new wallpaper."

Mrs. Zucker smiled. "She picked it out all by herself."

"That's what I figured," Grandpa Nevelson mumbled.

"I bet you're both hungry," Mrs. Zucker said quickly. The wallpaper discussion was over.

Caroline's mother spread out the three trays on the dresser. She set a soup bowl and a small plate with a grilled cheese sandwich on each tray. The first tray was for Grandpa Nevelson. The second one was for Caroline. Then she carried the last tray over and sat on the edge of the bed near Grandpa Nevelson's chair.

While the grown-ups talked about the weather, the candy store, and what was going on at the hospital, Caroline thought about her friends at school. They were probably all asking Maria about the bike accident. She hoped Maria wouldn't tell them she had been scared. *Especially* not Duncan!

"What would you be doing if you were in

school right now?" Grandpa Nevelson asked her after he finished eating.

Caroline looked at the clock on her desk. "Lunch is over. The kids are probably out on the playground."

"Do you wish you were playing with them?" he asked.

It would be fun, Caroline thought. But how often did she get to have an indoor picnic in bed? She told him, "Maybe. But it's neat having lunch with you and Mom."

Her grandfather smiled so broadly that his eyes crinkled up. He reached into his pocket and pulled out a small paper bag. "I brought you something."

"A present? For me?" Caroline took it and tried to guess what was inside. It was flat, but it was the wrong size for a candy bar. She reached into the bag and pulled out a cardboard package of markers. They were hot pink, green, red and blue, and they were so bright that she bet they would glow in the dark. "Thanks, Grandpa! These are great! I really needed new markers. I'm not going to let Patricia or Vicki *touch* these," she told him.

"I bet you thought it was candy," Grandpa Nevelson said with a twinkle in his eye.

"When I stopped at the candy store to get your treats, your grandpa insisted on bringing you a present, too," Mrs. Zucker said.

Caroline wiggled her finger until Grandpa Nevelson bent closer to her. Then she threw her arms around his neck. "I love you, Grandpa Nevelson!"

Caroline sat up in bed when she heard the door slam downstairs. Her sisters were home! She had never missed them so much in her whole life.

"What happened in school today?" she asked Vicki and Patricia when they finally came upstairs.

"I got my spelling test back from last week," Patricia told her. "I got all the words right."

Of course, Caroline said to herself. According to Patricia, she always did things right. Either her sister was perfect, or else she kept her mistakes a secret.

"What else happened?" she asked.

"We played kickball in gym."

"Is that all?" Caroline was disappointed. She had been hoping for some really exciting news.

"Guess what Ricky Madison did?" Vicki didn't wait for Caroline to guess. "He tried to punch Billy Smith, but Billy ducked and Ricky hit Mandy in the nose!"

"That's terrible!" Caroline decided that Ricky Madison must be the Duncan Fairbush of the kindergarten class.

"I hope he got into big trouble," Patricia said.

41

Vicki nodded. "He had to go see the principal, and Mandy had to visit the nurse."

Then it got very quiet. Her sisters had run out of news. The three of them sat and looked at each other until Laurie Morrell called, "The brownies are ready!"

"See you later!" Patricia said to Caroline as she and Vicki raced out the door.

Caroline glared at her bandaged ankle. If she didn't have to sit with her dumb foot on a dumb pillow, she could be running downstairs to get some warm brownies, too. Her mouth watered just smelling them.

She was feeling very sorry for herself fifteen minutes later. Everybody seemed to have forgotten about her, including Laurie. They hadn't even brought her one brownie!

Suddenly Maria stuck her head in the doorway. "Hi—how are you feeling?" she asked.

"Maria!" Caroline cried. "I'm so glad you're here!"

Maria smiled. "I'm glad, too. Laurie gave me a plate of brownies." She put the plate down on one side of the bed next to Caroline, then dropped a pile of schoolbooks on the other side. "I brought your homework," she added.

"Gee, thanks," Caroline sighed as she began munching on a brownie.

"It's not bad," Maria told her. "There's only one page of math problems. And we have to

42

finish another chapter for reading by Thursday. We did a science experiment in class, but Mrs. Nicks said you didn't need to worry about it."

When Maria finally finished listing the schoolwork, Caroline tried to look on the bright side. "I suppose it could be worse. I'll have plenty of time to work on it tomorrow."

"What did you do today?" Maria asked around a mouthful of brownie.

"Well, I watched Lucy Hanson on the *Tom Sullivan Show*—"

"Oh, wow! Was she good?" Maria interrupted.

"She *looked* really cute, but he didn't let her sing, and he only talked to her for five minutes. After the show, I caught up on last week's reading assignment. Then Grandpa Nevelson and Mom had a picnic with me up here." She pulled her new markers from under the bedspread. "Grandpa gave me these. I drew for a while this afternoon."

"Lucy Hanson and the picnic sound fun," Maria said thoughtfully. "But the rest sounds kinda boring."

"It was. Tell me about school."

Maria took another brownie and sat on the floor. "Duncan made a big deal because you were absent. He tried to tell everybody you'd stayed home because of the stuff he said last Friday."

"What?" Then Caroline remembered the stupid argument about how fast Duncan could ride his bike. "Did he say I was afraid to come to school because I thought he wanted to race?"

Maria shrugged her shoulders. "Something like that. You know how Duncan is."

Caroline groaned. "Do I ever!"

"But he shut up when Mrs. Nicks said you'd been hurt in an accident," Maria went on. "Samantha asked if it was a car crash. Then Duncan and Kevin started saying disgusting things. . . ."

"Like what?"

Maria shuddered. "Like asking *where* the cars crashed and if there was a lot of blood."

"Gross! That's exactly the kind of stuff that would interest Duncan Fairbush!"

Downstairs, Caroline heard the doorbell ring. She wondered who it was, but Maria had more to tell her about what she'd missed.

"Michael Hopkins got a haircut over the weekend."

"How does he look?" Caroline asked dreamily. She thought Michael Hopkins was the cutest boy in the whole third grade.

"He looks even cuter than he did before," Maria told her.

44

Just then, Laurie came into the room carrying a box. "A nice boy left this present for you," she said to Caroline.

Caroline grinned. "Oh, neat!" Maybe being stuck in bed with a sprained ankle wasn't so bad after all.

"What boy?" Maria wanted to know.

"He didn't tell me his name." Laurie frowned, trying to remember what he looked like. "He was about your age, I guess, but taller than either of you. His blond hair was real short, and he had blue eyes—I think."

Maria and Caroline stared at each other. "It sounds like Duncan," Maria said.

"It *couldn't* be!" But Caroline couldn't think of any other boy who matched that description.

"This present can't be from Duncan," Maria declared. "It must be from someone else, and Duncan just delivered it."

Caroline was hoping that maybe the present was from Michael. And then she lifted the lid off the box. Something jumped out at her. It felt slimy as it brushed against her hand. "YUCK!" she yelled.

Laurie gasped.

"It's a *frog*!" Maria cried as it hopped across Caroline's bedspread.

"Get him, Laurie!" Caroline pleaded, trying to move away from the creature.

45

"Don't you like frogs?" Laurie asked.

"Outside. I like frogs *outside,* where they belong!"

Maria started to giggle. "He's looking at your wallpaper. I bet he thinks he *is* outside."

Laurie grabbed the frog before he could hop anywhere else. She dropped him back into the box and quickly shut the lid. "I'll let him go in the garden. Whoever gave you this frog must really like you, Caroline," she said with a smile.

"Like me? Only Duncan Fairbush would be mean enough to give me a present like this! He *hates* me!"

Laurie raised her eyebrows. "I don't know about that. When I was in third grade the boys only bothered the girls they really liked."

Maria and Caroline looked at each other. Together they cried, "Duncan?"

Then they fell over themselves laughing.

5

THE WAR OF THE ROSES

"I want to get out of bed," Caroline announced on Tuesday afternoon.

Grandpa Nevelson shook his head. "I don't think so, honey. The doctor said you shouldn't be on your feet until tomorrow."

"But I'm so *tired* of sitting in my room!"

He smiled. "I thought you liked your bedroom now that it looks like a summer garden in bloom."

"I'm bored," she told him. It was one o'clock. All of her homework was finished. There was nothing on television that she wanted to watch. And lunch was over. What was she going to do until Maria visited after school?

"Bored?" her grandfather repeated in his big voice. "Then I'm glad I came over again this afternoon. I think I know just how to take care of that."

He pushed his chair away from the bed. Then he stretched out his legs and rested his feet near the end of Caroline's bed. She giggled at the sight. Her mother would have a fit if she saw someone's shoes on the bedspread.

"Lie down, Caroline. I've got a story to tell you."

She relaxed against the pile of pillows behind her head. When Grandpa Nevelson started a story, a smart person got comfortable. His stories could last a long, long time.

"Have I ever told you about the time I was a forest ranger in Washington state?" he asked.

"Just about the fire." Vicki had been so scared when he described the giant flames that she had started to cry.

He rubbed his chin. "Well, I have other tales. It was July . . . no, it was August when we got the call. The Princess was in danger—"

"A real princess? In the forest?" Grandpa Nevelson had met a lot of interesting people, but he'd never mentioned a princess until now.

He sighed the way he always did when one of his granddaughters questioned him. "Of course, she was a real princess. She was on vacation and then someone locked her inside the Aquamarine Castle—"

"A *castle?* In Washington state?"

Grandpa Nevelson folded his arms across his chest. "If you don't believe me, I'll have to find some other little girl who wants to hear my story."

"No, Grandpa," Caroline said quickly. "Don't leave. I really want to hear it, honest."

He unfolded his arms and took a long breath. "Well, rescuing that princess was hard work, believe me. The castle was locked, of course, but that wasn't the biggest problem. It was guarded by a fierce grizzly bear!"

Caroline imagined a growling grizzly and shivered.

"How would you like to fight a grizzly?" Grandpa Nevelson asked in a low, rumbling voice.

"I'd hate it!" She stared at her grandfather, trying to picture him as a forest ranger facing a mean bear. "Were you scared?"

He shrugged. "Of course not! My partner Roger was nearly seven feet tall, and everyone knew he was the strongest, bravest man in the West."

Caroline's grandfather was almost six feet tall himself. It was hard to imagine someone a whole foot taller than he was.

"Roger and I hiked to the castle," Grandpa Nevelson continued. "I brought my rifle, but my partner had no weapon. We didn't get there until almost dark."

"And then you shot the grizzly?" Caroline guessed.

He shook his head. "Didn't need to. I just fired into the air to get his attention. When the bear noticed us, Roger showed his teeth and snarled. The grizzly was so scared that he turned tail and ran into the woods. We never saw him again."

Caroline clapped her hands in delight.

"I'm not done yet," her grandfather told her. "We still had to free the princess. Roger marched right up to the castle and kicked down the door, and the beautiful blond princess ran to meet us."

Caroline said, "I bet she was glad to see Roger."

Her grandfather grinned. "Actually, she kissed *me*!"

"But Roger did all the work!"

There was a twinkle in his eyes as he explained, "But I was better-looking!"

Caroline laughed and laughed. Grandpa Nevelson told the best stories in the whole world! "You're really special," she told him.

"So are you, sweetheart," her grandfather said. A beeper sounded and he checked his watch. "Uh-oh—I've got to get back to the candy store. Will you be all right if I leave you? Your mother will be home from the hospital soon."

"If you lock all the doors, I'll be fine." Caroline yawned. "I think I'll take a nap."

"Another nap? What a sleepyhead you're turning into," he teased.

"I didn't sleep very much last night," she told him. "My ankle hurt every time I moved. But it's lots better now."

"Then I'm going to tuck you in." Since Caroline was lying on top of her blankets, he covered her with the quilted bedspread. After he pulled it up to her chin, he kissed her cheek and said, "Sweet dreams, Caroline."

There was something familiar about the princess crying in the castle window. In her dream, Caroline tried to remember where she had seen the girl before. Was it Patricia? No ... it was Caroline herself with long, blond hair.

"Help! Someone, save me!" the princess yelled.

Suddenly, Caroline was no longer watching the scene—she was part of it. She *was* the princess in the castle. Something growled on the ground below. She leaned out of the window and looked down, and her heart skipped a beat. The noise was coming from a gigantic bear!

Then suddenly things began to change. The trees in the forest got fuzzy and turned into flowers—huge yellow and lavender flowers! They grew taller and taller until they were higher than the castle. Caroline heard a rustling sound, and a sweet scent filled her nose. It was such a strong, sweet smell that she started to feel sick. She blinked twice before she could believe her eyes. The flowers were marching toward her! They were surrounding the castle!

Then a humming sound caught her attention. Leaning way out of the window, she tried to see past the army of flowers. The hum turned into a deafening buzz, and she saw a giant bee flying toward her. She ducked as it flew over her head and into the room.

"Get out of here!" she screamed, but the bee just smiled at her. It began circling around her head.

The window was so high she couldn't jump out. Even if she tried, she would be attacked by the giant flowers. They were so close now that she could touch them if she reached out the window.

"Help! Grandpa Nevelson! Save me!" Caroline shouted.

But Grandpa Nevelson wasn't there.

A sudden light blinded her. One of the flowers grabbed her shoulder and started to shake her. She tried to slap it away.

"Caroline! It's me, your mother. Wake up, honey!"

"What?" Caroline mumbled.

"You're having a bad dream. Wake up. Everything's all right," her mother promised.

Caroline rubbed her eyes and opened them slowly, expecting to see her old candy cane wallpaper. But the candy canes were gone! The yellow and lavender flowers had taken over her room! She checked for bees, but she didn't see any. Still, when she sucked in a deep breath, the air seemed to be thick with the sickening, sweet smell of roses.

Mrs. Zucker brushed the bangs off Caroline's damp forehead. "It must have been a terrible nightmare."

"It was awful! They were chasing me!"

"Who was?" her mother asked.

Caroline felt silly saying she'd been attacked by giant flowers and a monster bee. She faked a smile. "It was just a dream. Never mind." She glanced at the flowers. They were over her head. They were on the wall beside her bed. And she could see more of them past her mother's shoulder. They were *everywhere.*

"If you're all right, I'm going to start dinner," Mrs. Zucker told her. "Would you like to come downstairs and eat with us tonight?"

Getting out of the room and away from the horrible flowers sounded wonderful. Caroline tried not to sound too excited when she said, "I'd love it! But I thought I couldn't walk until tomorrow."

Her mother smiled. "Your father can carry you downstairs. And you can prop your foot up on a chair."

"Great! How soon is dinner?"

Caroline wished her mother would say that dinner would be ready in five minutes. Instead, she said, "In about half an hour."

Another half-hour with the flowers! She hoped the daisies and roses wouldn't do anything awful to her before her father came to rescue her.

6

I'VE MADE A MISTAKE!

"You don't look very happy," Vicki said to Caroline later that evening. The Zuckers were seated around the kitchen table, having supper.

"*I'd* be happy if I'd gotten to stay home for two whole days," Patricia said. "Grandpa Nevelson visited her both days, and he even gave her a present."

Caroline pushed her string beans around her plate with her fork.

"Are you feeling all right?" her father asked. "You're not eating much of anything. Does your ankle hurt?"

"Would you like to lie down, honey?" her mother asked.

"I'm fine," she mumbled.

On the other side of the table, Patricia suddenly started to cough. Vicki slapped her on the back, but that only made Patricia cough harder.

"She's choking!" Mrs. Zucker cried.

Their father jumped out of his chair and rushed to Patricia. He wrapped his arms around her stomach and squeezed. Patricia stopped coughing immediately.

Caroline was sure there was nothing caught in Patricia's throat. A person who had been choking wouldn't stop coughing right away because his or her throat would still feel funny. Patricia had faked the scene because she was jealous of all the attention Caroline was getting. She liked it best when everyone was listening to her.

When her parents were sure Patricia was all right, they turned back to Caroline. Her mother said, "You're awfully quiet. Something must be wrong."

She simply couldn't tell them about her dream. Her sisters would laugh themselves to death if they knew she was afraid of flowers.

"Are you nervous about going back to school?" her father asked.

Caroline decided that sounded like a good excuse. She nodded. "Yeah, that's it."

Her mother frowned. "I thought you finished all your homework."

"I did, but . . ." Now that Caroline was thinking about going back to school, she wasn't very happy about it. She'd have to sit out during gym class and recess. She'd have to copy somebody's notes from the science experiments she had missed. And everybody was going to ask about the accident.

She tried not to think about Duncan Fairbush, but she couldn't help it. He was going to say stupid things and that would make her mad.

Mrs. Zucker turned to her husband. "Do you think perhaps Caroline should stay home one more day?"

"No!" Caroline cried. Staying home with the flowers would be worse than facing Duncan.

Her mother raised her hands in the air. "Okay. If you feel so strongly about going back to school tomorrow, you can do it."

"Good!" Caroline gave a sigh of relief and began eating her dinner. Now all she had to do was get through the night.

Several hours later, Caroline opened her eyes in the darkness and pulled a flashlight from beneath her blanket. She aimed the flashlight at the clock on her desk. It said two o'clock. Then she pinched herself in the arm to make sure she was truly awake.

Slowly she moved the light around the room. The lavender daisies and yellow roses almost seemed to come alive in the shadows. Caroline began to remember all the things people had said about her wallpaper.

If you choose it, you have to live with it.
It's really ugly.
It's . . . interesting.
It's . . . colorful.

Her father had even said it reminded him of his Grandmother Zucker's house. Now that she thought about it, Caroline remembered hearing stories about Grandmother Zucker. She was the kind of woman who thought children should be seen and not heard. She didn't even believe in dessert! Caroline didn't like having a room like one of hers.

Maria had said the wallpaper might "grow on her" after a while. But Caroline had lived with it since Friday. She had spent almost all of the last two days and nights surrounded by the wallpaper, and it wasn't growing on her. Instead of liking it more as time went by, she was beginning to hate it.

When Caroline looked at the flowers in the shadows, she could imagine them peeling off the wall and sneaking toward her. When she heard a scratching noise, she nearly jumped out of her skin. Then she heard a familiar groan. "Baxter?"

The Zuckers' sheepdog-and-something-else mutt groaned again at the side of her bed. She

hadn't heard him come up to her room, but it was nice knowing she wasn't alone.

She patted her quilt and whispered, "Come here, Baxter."

The huge dog was happy to leap onto the bed. He didn't leave much room for Caroline, and it didn't feel very good when he leaned on her ankle. Still, she felt safer having him close to her. If any nasty flowers tried to grab her during the night, Baxter would protect her.

But even with Baxter at her side, Caroline couldn't sleep. It was hard to admit it, but everyone else had been right about the wallpaper and she had been wrong—very wrong.

And now she had to live with the lavender daisies and the yellow roses. How was she ever going to do it?

7

PEG-LEG GETS AN IDEA

"Heard you fell off your bike," Duncan said the second Caroline limped into their classroom the next morning. "What happened? Did you ride farther than the edge of your driveway and have a problem?" he asked with a nasty grin.

"I told you we were racing down the hill to the park," Maria said, coming over to stand next to Caroline.

"And I didn't believe you," he told her.

"It's true." Caroline glared at him.

He shoved his hands into his jeans pockets. "What hill?"

"Mountain Road."

"Mountain Road?" Duncan's mouth fell open.

"Are you impressed?" Caroline asked.

"Gimme a break, Zucker," he snarled.

In spite of what Duncan said, Caroline thought he *looked* impressed. She bet *he* had never raced down Mountain Road.

"That's a huge hill," Duncan said. "There's no way you raced down it."

Maria looked at Caroline in mock surprise. "Oh, no? Then where *were* we racing?"

"It *was* Mountain Road," Caroline told everyone who was listening. "If you don't believe me, ask the lady who lives in the pink house halfway down the hill."

Maria added, "Just find the huge bump in the sidewalk that made Caroline's bike flip. It's right in front of that house."

"Your bike flipped?" Michael Hopkins asked.

Caroline noticed his new haircut. She thought it looked very good. "I don't know if it flipped," she said. "I was too busy sliding across the sidewalk."

"*I* saw it," Maria said. "It happened right in front of me. It was *awful!*"

Samantha Collins squeezed next to Caroline. "Can I see your ankle?"

"Sure." She tugged her pant leg up until the elastic bandage showed.

"Is that all?" Samantha tossed her head, making her long, blond hair fly out. "I thought you'd have a cast on your leg or something."

"That's no big deal," Duncan said, trying to

63

make the kids pay attention to him. He started to push up his shirt sleeve.

"Are you going to show us your dumb scab *again?*" Samantha asked. "We've already seen it a million times!"

Caroline giggled. Was Duncan really jealous that she had been hurt worse than him?

"What's so interesting, class?" Mrs. Nicks asked as she came into the room. When she saw Caroline she smiled and said, "It's so nice to have you back at school, Caroline. I hope your ankle is feeling better."

"Much better, thank you," Caroline said, limping to her desk.

"Peg-Leg," Duncan whispered as she hobbled past him.

She felt her face getting hot. If he was going to call her Peg-Leg all day, she would use her *good* leg to trip him on the way to the playground!

By the time they went outside for recess, Duncan had forgotten all about Caroline. Kevin had been sent to the principal's office for making rude burping noises during art, and all the boys couldn't wait to meet him on the playground and find out what Principal Fletcher had done to him.

When Caroline and Maria joined Samantha and the other girls by the swings, everyone got quiet. Caroline had a feeling they had been talking about her.

"We heard you redecorated your room," Samantha said finally.

"I only got new wallpaper, that's all," Caroline said. "I didn't get new furniture or anything."

"What's it like?" Barb wanted to know.

"It's . . ." Caroline wondered what she could say about her wallpaper. It was interesting? It was colorful? It was making her crazy?

"It has lots of flowers on it," Maria said for her.

"You've seen it?" Samantha asked. Maria nodded, but she didn't say anything else. Everyone probably thought she was trying to keep Caroline's new wallpaper a secret.

The playground assistant blew her whistle—it was time for the class to go back into the building. Caroline was grateful to be rescued from the wallpaper discussion. As she limped along behind the other girls, she was surprised to find Duncan waiting for her.

"Did you get my present?" he asked her with one of his nastiest grins.

Caroline raised her eyebrows. "Present? Oh, you mean the frog?"

"Yeah." He grinned even wider. "I bet you screamed when you opened the box. I wish I could have been there!"

"Why would I scream? It was just a frog," she lied. He was never going to find out he had scared her.

"Boy, Zucker, you're not much fun," he told her. "Where's my frog now?"

Caroline smiled sweetly at him. It was her big chance to get even with Duncan for the hundreds of mean tricks he was always playing on her. "We had frog legs for dinner last night."

His face went pale. "Really? You're kidding, aren't you, Peg-Leg?"

"Of course I'm kidding. Two skinny frog legs couldn't feed five people." But Caroline wasn't about to stop teasing him yet. She *hated* being called Peg-Leg. "I fed him to my dog."

Duncan swallowed hard. "Geez," he said in a small voice. "I kinda liked that frog."

Caroline actually felt sorry for him then. But she waited until they were almost back to their classroom before she told him the truth. "I didn't really. The frog's living in my backyard."

"Great!" Duncan smiled. "Could I have him back?"

"No!" Caroline said. "You gave him to me, remember? He's *my* frog now!"

Caroline hurried home right after school. "Hi, Laurie," she called, hobbling as fast as she could toward the stairs to her attic room.

"Hold on a minute," Laurie said. "How was your day? Does your ankle hurt?"

Instead of answering, Caroline pointed to her bookbag. "I've got *tons* of schoolwork. Mrs. Nicks didn't send it all home with Maria—she saved some of it so she could give it to me in person."

She could not look Laurie in the face, because she wasn't exactly telling the truth. Although she had a little extra homework, that wasn't why she was in such a hurry to go upstairs. She had a different plan for the rest of the afternoon.

Laurie patted her on the shoulder. "Don't let me keep you from your work. Just try to stay off your feet. Give your ankle a rest."

"Okay."

But Caroline didn't stay off her feet. She dug into her desk drawers, looking for the posters she'd been saving. Then she climbed on her desk chair and began hanging them on the walls. Her plan was to cover the flowers. If she couldn't see them, maybe she could forget about them.

But her posters only covered half of the biggest wall, the one behind her desk. Caroline started cutting pictures out of magazines and taped them to the wall next to her bed. When she found a centerfold with Roddy Hastings's face, she taped that to the ceiling right over her

67

bed. She'd rather fall asleep looking at him than at the flowers.

Baxter padded into the room as she finished her project, and Caroline scratched him behind the ears as she checked her work. Two walls still needed to be covered—the one behind the head of her bed and the one opposite it. And flowers still peeked from between the posters and pictures on the other walls.

"It didn't work, Baxter," she sighed.

He looked up at her with his big, brown eyes and sighed, too, as if he was sorry her plan had failed.

"What am I going to do? Even if I tell Mom and Dad I hate the flowers, I can't ask them to buy me different wallpaper." She stopped scratching Baxter's ears, and he rubbed against her for more attention.

Caroline patted his head while she thought about her problem. She wished she could rip the flowered paper right off the walls, but she knew that would make a huge mess. And it would take forever to save up her allowance so she could buy enough posters to cover every single lavender daisy and yellow rose.

"Any ideas?" she asked the dog.

Baxter barked. If he was trying to give her a suggestion, she didn't understand it.

Then Caroline had an idea of her own. Nothing would cover the walls as well as paint! She could just imagine the flowers disappearing under a coat of bright, pretty paint. It was the perfect solution to her problem.

"But where will I get the paint?" she wondered out loud. "And when can I do it?" She tried not to listen to the even harder question inside her head: How was she ever going to get away with it?

8

CAROLINE'S BIG CHANCE

At ten o'clock on Saturday morning, Mrs. Zucker hung up the phone in the kitchen and said to her daughters, "I can't believe it! The schedule got mixed up at the hospital—I'm supposed to be at work right now! But your father is coaching the track team and he won't be home until early afternoon. What am I going to do with the three of you?"

Vicki looked at Patricia. Patricia looked at Caroline. And Caroline had an idea. "I can take care of things here."

"Maybe I could call Laurie," Mrs. Zucker said as if she hadn't heard Caroline. She reached for the telephone.

"But she had a big date last night," Caroline told her mother. "I bet she's sleeping late this morning. I can baby-sit Patricia and Vicki. Really!"

Her sisters liked the idea. Patricia said, "Let her do it."

"Yeah." Vicki hugged Little Pillow, the ratty old baby pillow that she used to take everywhere. Now she just slept with it, but on Saturdays she kept it with her until her favorite television cartoons were over.

Mrs. Zucker looked at Caroline. "You *have* done a good job when I've left you with your sisters for a short time. . . ."

"If anything happens, I could get Mrs. Heppler from across the street," Caroline told her.

"That's true." Their mother thought for another minute. Then she smiled. "Okay. You're in charge, Caroline. Now, I've got to get ready."

Caroline followed her mother into her bedroom. She got Mrs. Zucker's white nurse's shoes out of the closet while her mother slipped into her uniform. She dashed into the kitchen to look for the car keys when her mother couldn't find them in her purse.

"Thanks for all the help," Mrs. Zucker told Caroline five minutes later, when she was ready to leave.

"I like to help." Caroline opened the door for her mother.

Mrs. Zucker gave her a quick, curious look. "If I didn't know better, I'd think you were in a hurry to get me out of here."

That was exactly what Caroline was trying

to do. What if her mother changed her mind and called Laurie Morrell?

But Mrs. Zucker had no time to make different plans. She blew kisses to all three girls and ran to the car.

Caroline stood at the window and watched until the blue station wagon turned the corner. Then she smiled at her sisters. "How would you like to paint my room?"

Vicki clapped her hands. "I love to paint! Can I bring my new water colors? I can draw a good tree."

"I didn't ask you to paint *in* my room," Caroline explained. "I want you to help me *paint* my room. I'm tired of those old flowers."

Patricia stared at her for a long time. Caroline expected her sister to ask *why* she'd suddenly gotten tired of them—and there was no way Caroline was going to admit she'd made a mistake when she chose her wallpaper.

But Patricia just asked, "Where do we start?"

Caroline was surprised that Patricia hadn't laughed at her, or even said I-told-you-so. With a smile, she answered, "Let's start in the basement."

Caroline led the way to the steps, feeling like a general leading her soldiers. Downstairs, they started looking for paint cans.

Vicki found a tiny one. "Here's some."

Caroline read the label on the front. "This is

the shiny stuff Dad used to paint the window ledges. I don't think there's enough of it to cover my walls."

"There's not enough of *anything* to paint your whole room," Patricia said, picking up a paint can in each hand.

Ten minutes later, the girls were upstairs in Caroline's room. They had found four cans of water-based paint. One was light blue, one was purple, one was green, and one was black.

Caroline said, "We need to move my furniture out of the way. The posters and pictures have to come down. And we mustn't get any paint on my windows."

"I can do the posters," Vicki offered.

"Good idea."

Vicki grinned. She loved feeling important.

"Can you help me move my bed away from the wall?" she asked Patricia. "Mom will have a fit if we get purple or black spots on my bedspread."

Patricia looked at her sister as if she thought Caroline had gone crazy. "Do you think Mom's only going to worry about spots on the bedspread? Both Mom and Dad are going to have a fit when they see what we're doing!"

Caroline giggled. "That's why we have to finish before they get home. They can't do anything about it if the painting's already done." She asked herself, what was the worst thing they could do to her? Ground her in her bedroom for the rest of her life? At least she wouldn't be staring at the flowers, and the flowers wouldn't be staring back.

Soon the furniture was in the middle of the room, and the walls were bare. Caroline announced, "It's time to paint!"

"Wait!" Vicki cried. "I have to get my art shirt."

"Me, too."

Both sisters ran downstairs to their own room. Caroline didn't have an art shirt at home. Hers was buried in her desk at school. But she knew just what to use to cover her clothes. She hurried to her parents' room and found a worn-out old sweat shirt on the closet floor. Her father wore it for all his dirty projects, so it was covered with paint and grease spots. When Caroline tugged it over her head, it hung down to her knees.

Once they were all prepared, Caroline opened the can of light blue paint. "Let's start with the short wall where my bed belongs."

"What about Justin and Esmerelda?" Vicki asked. "What if we get paint in the fishbowl?"

"That would be a disaster." Caroline carefully moved the fishbowl to a small table out in the hall.

Patricia poured some paint into the mixing

pan and then dipped her roller into it. "I haven't seen this color in the house," she said.

"The bathroom walls were this color when you were a little baby," Caroline told her, getting some paint on another roller.

The blue went onto the wallpaper easily. But Vicki was the first to notice that the flowers still showed.

Caroline took three steps back to get a good look at the wall. Sure enough, she could see the outline of the daisies and roses. "Maybe the paint will get darker when it dries," she said hopefully.

They finished the short wall under the eaves quickly. Then Patricia looked up at the slanted ceiling. "What about those flowers?"

"We can't reach them," Caroline said. "I guess we could paint the part of the ceiling closest to the floor. But it would look weird if only half the wallpaper was covered."

"You're just going to leave those flowers?" Patricia asked. "You're right—it'll look weird."

"I'll cover them with a blanket or something," Caroline told her. Getting rid of all the flowers was harder than she had expected.

They decided to paint the next wall purple. No one knew where that paint had been used before in their house. Caroline thought the black looked great around the closet door. Only the green paint was left for the fourth

wall. Caroline painted that one herself—she didn't quite trust her sisters with that project.

She had to be very careful not to drop any paint on the furniture. Patricia and Vicki worked together on the other walls. Vicki painted the bottom half while Patricia stood on a chair and painted the higher part.

"We're done!" Vicki cried at last.

Caroline rocked back on her heels and frowned. "Hmmm . . ."

"Don't you like how it looks?" Patricia asked.

"It's . . . *interesting,*" Caroline said, using Maria's word. The flowers still peeked through the light blue paint, but the black paint covered everything. And the purple and the green actually looked pretty good.

"What was that?" Patricia asked suddenly. "I thought I heard a car. Is Dad home?"

Caroline peered out her window. "Yes. It's him! We've got to clean up this mess fast!"

9

CAUGHT!

"What's going on here?"

Mr. Zucker's deep voice made Caroline, Patricia and Vicki jump. They had been working so hard to straighten up Caroline's room that they hadn't heard him come up the stairs.

Caroline swallowed hard when she saw the look on her father's face. His eyes were narrowed as he inspected the room from the doorway. His lips were drawn together in a tight line. As she watched, his whole face began to turn red.

Vicki trotted over to him and gave him her cutest grin. "Hi, Daddy! We've been painting!"

When he looked down at her, Mr. Zucker started to laugh. Caroline wondered what was so funny. Then she noticed a splotch of green paint on the end of Vicki's nose. It made her look like a little elf.

"It looks as though you've all been very busy," he said. He didn't sound mad anymore. "Where's your mother?"

"She had to go to work," Caroline explained. "She didn't have time to get a baby sitter, so I said I'd do it."

"*You're* the baby sitter?" He raised his eyebrows. "Whose idea was it to paint your room?"

"Mine," Caroline mumbled.

Her father started to laugh again. He laughed so hard that he had to lean on the door frame to hold himself up. Then he quickly moved away. "Is this paint still wet?"

"No," Caroline told him. "It dries real fast."

Just then Baxter galloped up the steps and into the room. He almost knocked Mr. Zucker down. Baxter began barking and running around in circles, eager to find out what was going on.

When Caroline had calmed the dog down, her father said, "You know, Caroline, this paint job is an improvement. Those flowers were really awful."

"You're not angry?" Caroline could hardly believe her luck. "Not even about the money you spent on the wallpaper?"

"I think maybe you learned a lesson," he said.

Caroline stared at the floor. "Maybe. I guess I learned to listen to other people's advice."

"And maybe you also learned not to be so stubborn?" her father suggested.

"I'll try to be better," Caroline promised. But she couldn't help thinking that sometimes a nine-year-old had to be stubborn when grown-ups didn't want to listen to her.

"Do you need any more help in here?" Mr. Zucker asked.

Caroline was amazed. She'd expected him to yell at her, or at least ground her for the day, but he actually wanted to help! She pointed to the light blue wall. "The paint didn't exactly hide all the flowers."

"You're right—I still see some of those daisies and roses. But I have an idea. Be back in a minute."

As Mr. Zucker left the room, Patricia said, "If we'd painted *our* room, Daddy probably would have had a fit."

"Not if Vicki was there to make him smile," Caroline told her. She hugged her little sister. "Thanks for being so cute that Dad couldn't stay mad at us."

"Don't *I* get any thanks?" Patricia put her hands on her hips. "I don't like being left out!"

Caroline hugged Patricia, too. "Both of you were great today. I couldn't have painted the whole room without you!"

A few minutes later, their father returned with another paint bucket and a clean brush. He crossed the room and touched the light blue wall with one finger. "It's dry enough for me to paint over it if you want me to," he told Caroline.

"Oh, I do! What color is that?" she asked as he pried the lid off the can.

Mr. Zucker put a stick into the pail and stirred. "It's a much darker blue. I think it will look all right with the other walls, and it should take care of the flowers for good."

Caroline threw her arms around his waist. "Thanks, Dad! You're so smart!"

"I do my best," he told her with a smile. It didn't take him very long to repaint the short wall. Vicki waved good-bye as the roses and daisies disappeared one by one, and Caroline gave a sigh of relief.

"Did you want to leave the flowers on the ceiling over your bed?" her father asked Caroline.

"No way! But none of us could reach."

"I can take care of that, too." He went downstairs again and came back with a ladder. A big canvas drop cloth was draped over his shoulder and he was carrying a small can. When he put the can on her desk, Caroline tried to read the label, but it was smeared. She waited impatiently while her father spread the canvas over the floor and her bed to protect them from dripping paint. Then he set up the ladder and got to work.

"Ooh! It looks like night in here," Vicki cried when the ceiling was the same dark blue as the wall.

Mr. Zucker climbed off his ladder and took the small can from Caroline's desk. "I thought it might. That's why I brought this."

"What is it?" Caroline stood on her toes, trying to peer inside the can.

"Sparkle paint," he told her.

"Like the glitter people put on their clothes?" Patricia asked. "Susie Hall has a sweat shirt with a sparkly tiger on the front."

"It's something like that," her father explained. "When one of the nurses at the hospital was having a baby, your mother used this stuff to paint decorations for the baby shower. She didn't need the whole can, so she brought it home. She thought it might come in handy someday, and now it has."

"What are you going to do with it?" Caroline asked. She was so curious she could hardly stand it.

"Don't you like surprises?" Mr. Zucker teased as he climbed the ladder again.

He pulled a very small brush out of his hip pocket and dipped it into the paint can. Then he started touching the bristles here and there to the dark blue ceiling. To Caroline, it looked as if he was making a bunch of dots. She bit her bottom lip. Her father was smart, all right, but he wasn't an artist. What if he did something that looked even worse than the flowers?

She was still worrying when he put the lid on the paint can and came back down the ladder. He asked the girls, "Well, what do you think?"

Patricia frowned. "What is it?" she asked.

Mr. Zucker suggested, "Stand right underneath the ceiling and look up."

All three girls crowded next to the ladder and tipped their heads back. Caroline sucked in her breath. It was too wonderful! Her ceiling looked like a night sky filled with twinkling stars.

Vicki clapped her hands. "It's beautiful, Daddy! I never saw so many stars!"

"They even sparkle." Patricia sounded jealous. "I wish we had stars on the ceiling of *our* room. You sure are lucky, Caroline Zucker!"

"Is everything done now?" Mr. Zucker asked after all the furniture was back in place.

"One more thing." Caroline ran into the hall and got Justin and Esmerelda's bowl. Then she put it on the table where it belonged. "There! *Now* we're done!"

"Everyone is going to love your room now," Vicki said.

"Even Mom?" Patricia asked.

"Mom?" Caroline's heart started pounding. She looked at her father. "Uh, Dad, could *you* tell Mom what we did with my room?"

Mr. Zucker sat down on the edge of her bed. "Why can't you tell her?"

"She'll understand better if she hears it from you," Caroline said. She was afraid that her mother would never leave the girls home alone again after she found out what they had done.

Her father took her hands and held them between his bigger ones. "I think you ought to tell her yourself, sweetie. You're a big girl now."

Caroline pulled her hands away. "Then I have to find some blankets. Will you help me hang them over my walls?"

He cocked his head to one side. "You plan to *hide* the walls rather than tell her you changed your mind about the wallpaper?"

"I won't hide them forever," she told her father. "But Mom will be tired after work. She might be feeling crabby. I'll tell her when she's in a better mood."

Mr. Zucker grinned. "Don't you think your mother might ask why there are blankets hanging on your walls?"

Patricia and Vicki giggled. Caroline stared at her feet. "I guess you're right," she said with a sigh. "I'll have to tell Mom as soon as she gets home."

10

HOW LUCKY CAN YOU GET?

"Tell me what?" Mrs. Zucker asked, coming into the room. Before anyone could answer, she had another question. "What on earth happened in here?"

"Hi, Marsha." Mr. Zucker got up and went over to her. Then he gave her a kiss.

Patricia groaned and mumbled, "Mushy stuff."

But Vicki smiled. "I think it's nice."

Their mother slowly walked around the room, looking at each wall. Finally she said, "This is just what I needed!"

"What's that supposed to mean?" Caroline asked nervously. Her mother wasn't frowning, but she wasn't smiling, either.

Mrs. Zucker sat on the desk chair and stretched her legs out in front of her. "It was a rough day at work, and I was pretty tired when I came home. But this . . ." She waved her hand toward the walls and the sparkling ceiling. "This is just what I needed to cheer me up!"

Caroline blinked. "You *like* it?"

"It's quite an improvement over those awful flowers." She smiled at Mr. Zucker. "Don't you agree?"

"Absolutely!" He pointed to the stars. "I have to admit I helped with some of this redecorating project."

Mrs. Zucker shook her head, pretending to be upset. "I just can't leave any of you alone. But the next time you want to paint, dear, the kitchen could really use some work."

"What color would you like it to be?" he asked.

"Peach or ivory," she said promptly. "But just *one* color, please. Caroline is the only one who needs a room with more colors than a rainbow."

"You really like my room now?" Caroline asked. She still couldn't quite believe that her mother wasn't angry.

Mrs. Zucker looked around again. "I'm not thrilled by that black wall. It's so . . . *black.*"

"That's why I used the black paint on the wall with the closet," Caroline explained. "There isn't very much wall because of the door."

"But there's a big space between the closet

and the corner." Her mother stared at the spot for a moment. Then she snapped her fingers. "It's just about the same size as . . ."

"As what?" Patricia wanted to know.

"Matt, do we still have that old full-length mirror in the basement?" Mrs. Zucker asked.

Mr. Zucker nodded. "I saw it when I got the ladder."

"Would it fit in that space?"

He tried to measure the area with his hands. "I think it would, but there's only one way to know for sure. I'll go get it," he said as he left the room.

"A full-length mirror?" Caroline was excited. She loved the idea of having a big mirror in her room. Every morning after she got dressed she'd be able to check her entire outfit. She could see all of herself instead of just her head and shoulders.

"Can I use it sometimes?" Patricia asked her.

Caroline thought about that. "Maybe if you walked Baxter more often, I'd let you share it," she said. "I guess we could work something out."

"You mean I'll have to do some of your chores or you won't let me look in your dumb mirror?" Patricia pouted and folded her arms across her chest.

"Girls!" their mother said. "The mirror isn't

even up yet. Let's see if it fits before you start arguing over it."

"Watch out! Here I come," Mr. Zucker warned from the hall. He came into the room holding the long, heavy mirror in front of him.

"It's so *big!*" Vicki said, and Caroline smiled. Most things were bigger than little Vicki.

"I need some help over here," their father called as he tried to hold the mirror up against the wall.

All the girls ran over to help him. Vicki grabbed the bottom edge of the mirror, Patricia held onto one side and Caroline helped with the other.

Mr. Zucker asked, "How does it look?"

"Who knows?" Mrs. Zucker said, laughing. "I can't see anything except the four of you!"

"I think it fits," he said. "Let's put it down now—gently. Very gently."

Caroline, Patricia and Vicki helped him ease the mirror down until it was resting on the floor and leaning against the wall. "I'll get a hammer and some nails and hang it up later."

"Not now?" Caroline asked, disappointed.

Her father shook his head. "Not now. I'm tired. This redecorating project has worn me out!"

Mrs. Zucker took his hand and led him toward the door. "Me, too." She told the girls, "We're going downstairs to rest."

When their parents were gone, Patricia and Vicki wandered around Caroline's room. Patricia spent a long time making faces at herself in the mirror. Vicki stood under the stars and stared up at them. "I don't know anyone else in the whole world who has stars on their ceiling," she said.

"Or walls that are four different colors," Patricia added.

"Isn't it neat?" Caroline felt very happy and proud. She loved her new room. The flowered wallpaper had made her feel as if she was living in a horrible nightmare. But now the nightmare was over. She knew in her heart that she *belonged* in the room with blue and purple and green and black walls, and the stars on the ceiling.

"It's the neatest room I ever saw," Vicki said.

"Maybe I could help you guys with *your* room," Caroline offered.

Vicki moved closer to Patricia and whispered something into her ear. Patricia nodded. Then she said, "Thanks, Caroline. But we like the bunnies on our walls. We don't want to cover them up with anything, not even sparkly stars."

For the first time since Tuesday afternoon, Caroline was eager to go to bed that night. There would be no flowers to sneak up on her while she slept. She wouldn't have to shine her flashlight on the walls to check for spiders and snakes and huge bumblebees.

She pulled the quilt under her chin and gazed at the ceiling above her. The moonlight shining through her window made the stars twinkle. And when she turned her head, she saw the glittering stars reflected in the mirror that her father had hung on the wall after dinner. It looked so wonderful that she tingled right down to her toes.

It was really amazing how she'd finally gotten a room she could love, Caroline thought. Patricia and Vicki had helped her paint the walls, even though they knew they might get into trouble. Her father had been super—covering the light blue paint, making the stars, and hanging the mirror. And her mother had been the biggest surprise of all. She hadn't gotten mad for even a second, and she'd been the one who suggested the mirror.

Everyone in the family had helped. (Well, maybe Baxter hadn't done much. But he had stayed out of the way while they were all working, and that was good enough.) Caroline was sure she couldn't have done it by herself. When she looked around her room, it was even more special because she knew which person had helped with which thing.

Everybody had made a big fuss over her

when she had to stay in bed. And no one had made fun of her when she'd decided that she hated the flowered wallpaper.

Caroline smiled into the darkness and the twinkling stars seemed to smile back at her. She was lucky to be Caroline Louise Zucker. And she was even luckier to be part of the nicest family in the whole world!